"About the importance of being an Irish play!"
-Oscar Wilde

How to Write an Irish Play

John Grissmer

authorHOUSE®

AuthorHouse™
1663 Liberty Drive
Bloomington, IN 47403
www.authorhouse.com
Phone: 833-262-8899

Published by AuthorHouse 07/23/2020

ISBN: 978-1-7283-6720-0 (sc)
ISBN: 978-1-7283-6719-4 (e)

Print information available on the last page.

This book is printed on acid-free paper.

CAST BREAKDOWN

Here's the Cast Breakdown:

CLYDE, An Irish guy, any age, he functions as the chorus, Master of Ceremonies, Main Narrator. Plays different roles at different times.

MICK, Middle-aged owner of the Pub, the Horse's Glass. We suspect him of murdering his wife and her lover.

FR. TOM, Catholic priest, late 60s, with not a quick mind. Winds up in Heaven as a saint.

GROGAN O'BRIEN, A Ford dealer, red-faced, age 58. Not too bright, but not exactly dumb either. Father of:

GROGAN O'BRIEN, JR., A blandly pleasant young man in his mid-30s, known as JR, he falls tragically in love with ANNA.

ANNA, An attractive leading lady, rich voice, strong presence. She is also the Goddess Dramanesta.

THE PLOT/STORY, on a single set, the interior of the Horse's Glass, a run-down dump of a country pub on the southwest coast of Ireland. CLYDE, with the aide of the GODDESS DRAMANESTA creates a stunning, classic, Irish play.

ACT I

(Lights up on the interior of a pub called The Horse's Glass, located a half mile from the tall, sea coast rocks known as The Cliff's of Saint Seymour in south-western Ireland. The interior of this pub is ugly, rundown, dim and dirty. There is a main entrance door somewhere, a door to the back room behind the bar, and a door to a single toilet anywhere the designer wants to put it. CLYDE, an interesting looking ageless male actor, enters from that door. A loud flush sound is heard all over the theatre. CLYDE seems lost in thought. HE looks at his hands, carefully inspecting them.)

CLYDE

(To audience)

I forgot to wash me hands.

(HE starts back, stops, looks at his hands again,

and comes to a decision. HE speaks to the audience.)

Oh, well. As everyone knows and agrees, the finest plays being written today come from Ireland. Irish playwrights are acknowledged the world over as masters of the dramatic art. So therefore it is my intention tonight to take you for a walk through of a typical Irish play, to give you a close-up experience of the qualities which make Irish plays the bosses of the theatrical world. Like a surgeon, we're gonna take our scalpel to an Irish play, cut it open and see what makes it bleed.

Now first off, consider the playing area. You'll never find an Irish play set in a fancy French restaurant in Paris, that's for sure. And there are a lot of other places as well that are not going to be the setting for an Irish play. So never mind them. There are only two settings for your Irish play. The shadowy, run-down parlor in somebody's flat in Dublin. Or the grim, grimy, grungy-dirty, depressing, broken-down old country pub on the rocky southwest coast of Ireland, stuck out along a muddy back road where the constant sea wind whistles over the magical, misty green hills. Listen!

(Erie wind sound)

CLYDE (Cont.)

This here dismal setting is designed to contrast with the charming and compelling characters that are going to captivate and entrance you. For as you know, top dog characterization is the hallmark of an Irish play. I'm the best of the lot in this particular example. My name is Clyde, filling the role as your central narrator kind of fella. Extremely likable, I am, with a mysterious hint of brawny masculine energy about me that pulls women my way, but at the same time warns them off a wee bit. It's pretty clear there's much more to me than meets the eye, and that I've got some kind of dark secret lurkin' deep within me.

(MICK, who looks like MICK, enters from a door behind the bar. HE places bottles of whiskey on the shelves.)

MICK

That is such bullshit!

CLYDE

Could ya be more specific?

MICK

Brawny masculine energy?

CLYDE

Allow me to present himself, Mick the Publican and Landlord of The Horse's Glass.

(MICK waves dismissively to the audience.)

Mick is like the goalie in soccer, the back-stop, key player. The role looks easy, but the man who plays Mick must always be first-rate.

MICK

(Opening up the *Dublin Times*)

Give it a rest, will ya Clyde.

CLYDE

You'd think he was truly annoyed at me or something.

(MICK glares at CLYDE, then returns to his paper. Outer door opens and in comes FATHER TOM, a dignified priest of sixty who has an air of sadness about him.)

CLYDE

Ah, Father Tom. Good day to you Father Tom.

FATHER TOM

(Neutral)

Good day to you, Clyde.

(FATHER TOM sits at a table some distance from CLYDE. HE unfolds a newspaper and spreads it on the table. MICK automatically draws a pint and places it on FATHER TOM'S table.)

CLYDE

What's an Irish play without a priest? Dear old Father Tom, but you'll notice he has an air of indefinable sadness about him.

(FATHER TOM ignores CLYDE)

What terrible secret could be eating away at his guts, this world weary, holy man? I expect we'll find it out along about ten minutes before the final scene. And I can assure you all it won't be pretty.

(CLYDE studies MICK who ignores him. And then HE studies FATHER TOM who also ignores him.)

No it won't be pretty at all, at all. It'll make your skin creep.

(SILENCE from MICK and FATHER TOM)

(CLYDE clears his throat. Tries a new approach)

You may be wondering why there is not a lot of anything going on. Just Mick reading his paper; and Father Tom reading his paper. That's the true comfort of an Irish play ya see. The critics love you no matter what, and you don't need to have much of a story at all. Just captivating characters such as we are. And brooding atmosphere. So if any of you need to go to the bathroom, or to stick your nose out in the street for a smoke, go right ahead. You won't miss much. We'll still be here.

MICK

(Exploding)

All right, that's it! That's enough! I've had it. Out, Clyde! Get out!

FATHER TOM

Leave him be, Mick.

MICK

I can't take it anymore.

FATHER TOM

He does no harm.

MICK

He harms my equilibrium. Making me lose my temper and commit maybe a mortal sin of anger. What do ya think?

FATHER TOM

You're forgiven. 'Tis a very small sin anyway. Clyde, sit and have a drink with me.

MICK

No, he'll be having no drinks until we settle this.

CLYDE

(To the audience)

Now I wonder what it can be that is troubling Mick?

MICK

(Comes up beside CLYDE and scornfully imitates him.)

Oh, I wonder what can be troublin' Mick? Oh, dear, what in the world can be troublin' Mick? Can't you see what we all see? You are talking to a freaking wall. That there's a blank wall! There is no audience. The only audience is within your freaking feverish brain. I get so sick of this crapola you've dreamed up. It was mildly amusing the first hundred times you pulled it, Clyde. It was starting to annoy me the next hundred times, and now it has reached the place where I may give in to violence. It is no longer funny or cute, Clyde, or whimsically entertaining to see you pretending we're all actors on the stage of a god damn freaking theater! So stop it. No more of it! You hear me talking to you, Clyde, I mean it. Make an end to it! Now.

CLYDE

(Looks out at the audience for a long time. MICK retires behind the bar.)

I wonder what could be troublin' Mick?

MICK

I give up. I'm just going to have to split his skull with me regulator.

(He pulls a mean looking club from behind the bar)

FATHER TOM

Now, now, Mick. None of that. Pour me a jar and one for Clyde.

7

(MICK, still steamed, follows orders)

CLYDE

That is most commendable of you, Father Tom. Thank you kindly.

(CLYDE joins FATHER TOM at the table)

FATHER TOM

Now then____. How are ya, Clyde?

CLYDE

I'm feeling pretty fit, Father Tom.

FATHER TOM

Well it's pleased I am to hear that. Tell me one thing, Clyde, did you always have strong ambition to be an actor?

CLYDE

No, Father Tom, I can't say as I did at all.

FATHER TOM

Is that a fact? For then how does one account for this vast compulsion or illusion, whatever you want to call it, that we're all takin' part in some kind of play?

CLYDE

Didn't Shakespeare say something like that once, that we're all actors on the stage of life, something to that effect____?

FATHER TOM

Have you ever read Shakespeare?

CLYDE

No, but I think I heard that he said such a thing once on the television.

FATHER TOM

Shakespeare was on the television? How could that be?

CLYDE

No, no, no, they were like talkin' about Shakespeare on the television.

FATHER TOM

Oh.

MICK

You're making a big mistake, Father, taking him serious. Just ignore him, as I do.

FATHER TOM

I don't remember you ignoring him just now.

CLYDE

(To audience)

What is happening here? Why a scene of conflict is developing between Mick and Father Tom. About me?

MICK

Stop that.

CLYDE

Where will it lead?

MICK

I'm warning ya!

FATHER TOM

Catch a breath of air, Mick. Have a smoke. Here___

(He offers Mick a cigarette from a crumpled pack)

MICK

Thanks. I need a break from all the daftry going on here.

(MICK steps outside with a feeling of relief)

FATHER TOM

Clyde, tell me straight, are you all right with God?

CLYDE

How do you mean?

FATHER TOM

It's the sort of thing a priest is duty bound to ask. Are you luggin' some sinful burden of guilt?

CLYDE

What would I have to be guilty about, Father? You yourself hear all my sins, puny as they are.

FATHER TOM

Well, I'm not allowed to talk about that stuff, ya see — outside of confession.

CLYDE

I'm all right with God. As far as I know. I wonder if God's all right with me?

FATHER TOM

Here now, what kind of talk is that?

CLYDE

Merely speculating. It's the kind of intellectual exploration ya might expect to hear in a character exposition scene such as we're pickin' our way through here.

FATHER

I'm playing no scene, and that was a shameful kind of speculation — whatever ya meant by it. God forgive you, and I'm sure He does. But what I was getting at. Perhaps it would be the proper thing for you to see a friend of mine. A very able doctor____

CLYDE

I have no need for a doctor.

FATHER TOM

Clyde, he is a doctor of the mind.

CLYDE

You're saying what they call a shrink?

FATHER TOM

There's the flip word for it. But I'm dead serious here, Clyde. I fear this little game of yours is not too healthy for your good old brain.

CLYDE

(To audience)

And I fear a threat is developing here. I see it. They'll put me in the mental house. They'll drug me all to hell and stick electric prongs up my ass.

FATHER TOM

Stop that! All I'm asking is that you lay off your little game when Mick's around. You can see what it does to him.

CLYDE

Yeah, I'm very sorry about that. And I'm sorry about something else as well. I said they'll put electric prongs up my ass. The truth is they put the electric prongs on your head. I just said ass to get a cheap laugh. But it was dishonest. I'm surprised that a playwright of the caliber of Shawn Michael O'Mooney would lower himself to such a thing. Ya see, Father it been an established fact, well known for two and a half thousand years, that a sure way to get an audience in the theatre to laugh is to say piss, shit or fuck.

FATHER TOM

That'll be enough!

CLYDE

Arse or Ass works just as well. Or the variation. Asshole.

FATHER TOM

Clyde! Stop! Now I mean it!

CLYDE

Oh, don't you worry, Father. The critics will punish me well enough. I can just picture them out there in the dark, giving me a black mark for seeking an all too easy laugh with bad language. They'll see it as discommendable.

FATHER

Rightly so.

CLYDE

No, you can't put one by the critics. Don't even try. Ya know, Father, they are the brightest, most witty and intelligent practioneers in the whole writing game.

Overworked and underpaid are the critics. And unappreciated too, I think. Sometimes they may have to be a bit cruel, pointing out failures and shortcomings. But they are cruel only to be kind.

FATHER TOM

That gives me an idea, Clyde. If you think so highly of the critical game, why not become one yourself. I could have a word with Bill Flynn over at the weekly. He could send you to Dublin and you could write up stories on some of the shows there. What do ya think?

CLYDE

Ah, that's a pretty dream, Father.

FATHER TOM

(Returning to his paper)

Well, you'd be good at the job.

CLYDE

Naw, I lack for the education, and the savvy sensitivity. I'm nowhere near bright enough to be a critic. Still, I'm flattered that you could think of me that way at all.

MICK

(Comes back inside, goes behind the bar.)

The Grogan's just pulled up.

FATHER TOM

Ah, the Grogan's is it? Why I haven't seen them since___when was it___ only yesterday.

CLYDE

(To audience)

Grogan O'Brien and his son, Grogan Junior. Bitter conflict between the generations, is a well-established theme in Irish plays. Fathers and sons going after each other. Look out now!

(GROGAN O'BRIEN enters followed by his son, GROGAN O'BRIEN JR. who is known as JUNIOR. GROGAN senior is 68, red faced and healthy looking. JUNIOR is a blandly pleasant looking young man in his mid-thirties.)

GROGAN

Hello Mick.

MICK

Grogan. Hello Junior.

JUNIOR

Hello, Mick. Hello, Father Tom, Clyde.

CLYDE

Hello Grogan. Hello Junior.

GROGAN

Good day to you, Father Tom. Clyde.

JUNIOR

(Walks up to CLYDE, looks out into the audience)

So, how's the house look today?

CLYDE

It's a near sell-out. A discerning and appreciative audience, just about the best kind of people you could ever imagine.

JUNIOR

And especially the critics eh? Have you done that thing yet where you brown-nose the critics?

CLYDE

(Giving him a hurtful look)

I have no idea what yer referring to.

JUNIOR

Have it your way. I was only attemptin' to play along with yuz.

CLYDE

(Phony acting)

So___how is every little thing, Junior, between you and your old man? Your father. Your Daddy, your dear old Da?

JUNIOR

Fine. Couldn't be better.

CLYDE

Oh, ya don't say?

JUNIOR

I do say. (Turning sharply away from CLYDE) I'll have me usual, Mick____

CLYDE

(To the audience)

Ah, the hidden resentments, the buried memories of childhood horrors. The gut-wrenching revelations to come. But see now, on the surface, how everything is tranquil. Cute as a babbling brook on a sunny day in May.

MICK

(To GROGAN)

I forget, what's his usual?

JUNIOR

What I always have, Mick. Jamison, neat, with water on the side. Why is it you never fail to recall my Dad's usual, but you always forget mine?

MICK

(Because he doesn't know)

I don't know.

GROGAN

Let's not make a big thing out of it, boy.

(There is a pause of silence)

JUNIOR

It just seems odd, that's all. Should it not be a fundamental skill required in the Pub business? Regular customer. Your Publican ought to pour your usual automatic like, but he can't remember mine?

(Silence from all)

Am I that insignificant, Mick?

MICK

No, Junior, you're not that insignificant at all. To be honest I can't tell you why I usually forgot *your* usual. It's never troubled me 'til now.

JUNIOR

It's never troubled me either.

(HE takes his drink and sits with CLYDE. All are silent for a beat)

MICK

Have any of you met the American woman yet?

(ALL freeze except CLYDE who springs up, delighted.)

Ah, but I feel like handsprings and somersaults, with sprightly music in the air. The author, Shawn Michael O'Mooney, is a young school teacher from a tiny crossroads to the West of here. This is his very first play and there's a lot riding on it. His darling ancient mother is quite sick from the miseries of a life long and well lived. Shawn Michael seeks to make her final days, peaceful and happy with a few modest luxuries he will be able to afford should this play be successful. And he's well on the road as I see it. Now, did you notice with what a backhand flip Shawn Michael threw in a first mention of the pivotal character who will be a major force in the big dramatic mushroom that's about to spring up here?

MICK

Have any of you met the American woman yet?

CLYDE

Bravo, Shawn Michael O'Mooney. The situation and the characters are set out before us like a dinner table full of fine china and crystal and silver settings. And now here comes that outsider, the American woman to stir things up, like a fine steaming roast beef placed up on the table, with horse radish and mustard and greens and potatoes and vegetables, and bread and butter and salad with spicy dressing, and then dessert after all that maybe I'll only have a cup of tea, black brewed, lots of sugar. A dash of cream.

GROGAN

(To MICK)

Not only have we met her, but we have contracted to do business with her.

JUNIOR

She walked in yesterday, pretty as you please, and leased one of our top-line Ford SUV's for the week. For her property scouting, ya know.

CLYDE

Did I forget to mention? The Grogans are the dealers for Ford automotive products in our town. As they say, and how true it is. You can always depend on a Ford.

MICK

Property scouting, eh? It's true what I hear then? She and her husband are going to build some kind of high-tech factory, computer-type software sort of thing? And she's looking to pick up some old farmland from a family in hard circumstances, and them to be forced to sell cheap what is dear to them?

GROGAN

She's looking to buy some land. She told us that much.

JUNIOR

As for the rest of it, Mick, that about picking up old farmland from some family in hard circumstance and them forced to sell cheap what is dear to them. That's sort of an old-fashioned outlook. The Irish always whining about how they got exploited by the British first and now the Americans____ Come on, let's grow up. There's plenty of prosperity to go round these days. I'm sure she'll pay top dollar.

MICK

I've got nothing against her. Just speaking what I heard____.

CLYDE

(To audience)

(Holds up two fingers locked)

Irish and Americans. We're just like that. I believe that some happy day to come Ireland will be the fifty-first state of the United States of America. Ours will be the only green star in the flag. It will happen much sooner than you think. Anyhow, so here's what's coming, thanks to the crafty scheming of Shawn Michael O'Mooney. The American woman will be making her appearance. But not just yet. Oh, no. First we'll have to describe her, and then speculate a lot about her and her husband and what could be her real motive for bein' here, and what did she say, and what will she do, and then we'll have to get into an argument over our speculations. Ah, it'll be a grand and glorious battle. Insults will be flung about the room like dead fish.

GROGAN

Ah. Speak of the devil. Here she is now. She just pulled up.

CLYDE

Well, as I was saying____Change of plan____Here she comes now____. Although I should think Shawn Michael O'Mooney could have given us more time to discuss and digress over her before she makes her appearance. It's a bit disappointed I am.

(ANNA DUVAL enters. SHE is dynamic and good looking in her ripe mid-thirties. SHE carries a guide book with her finger marking a page. SHE takes a moment to gaze all around the room.)

ANNA

Well, look who's here. Hi ya, Junior. Hi ya, Grogan.

JUNIOR

Good day to you, Mrs. Duval.

GROGAN

May we stand you to a drink, Mrs. Duval.

ANNA

So this is it. The Horse's Glass. Sure, I'll have a pint of whatever. Please, call me Anna. Have you guys seen this guidebook? See here's a picture of this place.

JUNIOR

Well, so it is. What about it, Mick? Have you seen this?

MICK

Taken well before my time.

GROGAN

Mrs. Duval, may I present Mick, the Publican.

ANNA

A pleasure to meet you, Mick. Do you have a last name?

MICK

I forgot it long ago. What was it ya requested?

ANNA

A pint of whatever.

MICK

Oh, sure____. We've got plenty of that____

(He sets about drawing a pint)

JUNIOR

So, Mrs. Duval, what does it say in the guidebook?

ANNA

(Reads)

The Horses Glass, one of the last of a dying breed, an authentic back-country pub. A friendly, grimy, shambles of a place, having not a thing in common with the new slick Gourmet Brew Pubs springing up all over the landscape. The place is crawling with characters, and grubby atmosphere. Go there to enjoy the wit and wisdom of the sweetly grouchy old Publican, known only as Mick. He is said to have forgotten his last name.

(She shows the book to Mick)

See? But that's not you is it?

MICK

It's my father. Or could be my grandfather____

ANNA

(Looking around)

Well, this is certainly an old place.

FATHER TOM

It is that.

ANNA

You must be Father Tom. Hello, I'm Anna.

FATHER TOM

How did you know me?

ANNA

(Sitting at his table)

I'm not sure; I guess there's something about a priest that lights up my radar.

MICK

Can your radar also spot a crazy man?

(Pointing to CLYDE)

CLYDE

(Joining ANNA and FATHER TOM at the table)

Never mind. Never mind. It is indeed an honor to meet Anna, the central, inciting character of the drama. I am Clyde, as you must know from the study of your script.

FATHER TOM

I suppose you're going to tell me you used to be a Catholic. People are always telling me that. As though they're proud of it.

ANNA

Yeah? Well, I used to be a lot of things.

(To CLYDE)

Now then, what was it you said?

CLYDE

I was welcoming you to the play we're in. Here and now — on this stage — all of us here.

ANNA

What kind of a play is it?

CLYDE

It's a tragedy of course. A gritty Irish tragedy.

ANNA

Oh, well, sorry. I don't feel in the least bit tragic or gritty.

CLYDE

Give it time, we're only in the first act. Everything is delightful in the first act. Little do we know____

JUNIOR

Ah, never mind him. He's harmless daft.

CLYDE

Little do we know____

JUNIOR

(To CLYDE)

Stop that.

(To ANNA)

Tell us now, Anna, did you find any likely property in your explorations?

ANNA

Nothing so far, I'm afraid. I have a few leads to follow up, but____

(To FATHER TOM and CLYDE)

I suppose you've heard my husband and I are planning to build a factory here.

FATHER TOM

We've heard something of that.

JUNIOR

Say, Anna, I've an idea. How would you like to let me show you some farms and land and such, that are for sale? A fair distance from town, but they might be just what you're looking for. I would be happy to be your guide.

ANNA

That would be wonderful, Junior. Thank you. How about tomorrow morning?

GROGAN

Since when do you know what properties are for sale? I thought you were in the automobile business with me.

JUNIOR

(Ignoring his father)

Tomorrow morning then. It'll be grand. We'll drive out in the countryside. The weather will be fine. We'll take a picnic basket, with some tasty food and wine. We'll park the car under a welcoming tree, and there we'll be alone, you and me. We'll eat and drink and get to know each other well, my lovely lass, and then we'll spread a blanket on the grass____

GROGAN

Junior, what the hell are you talking? Mrs. Duval is a married lady.

JUNIOR

(Snapping out of it)

What was it?

CLYDE

All right, all right so now you've seen it plain in the face. Shawn Michael O'Mooney has this wee bit of a failing. He sometimes let his characters blurt out exactly what is on their minds and in their hearts. He calls it "honesty." It is really malpractice. The trick of the drama game is to conceal from the audience all the secrets of the plot until it comes time to reveal them. Not just vomit them up wily nilly. And in rhyme? Ugh! Now the whole conflicted relationship between Junior and Mrs. Duval has been prematurely exposed. I don't know what Shawn Michael could have been thinking.

ANNA

(To JUNIOR)

It was a charming speech, Junior. And in rhyme. I loved it. I am indeed in the land of the poets.

JUNIOR

No, I apologize. I lost control____

ANNA

Forget it. Come on, have a drink with us. Mick, pour him whatever he's having.

(GROGAN whispers to MICK as ANNA speaks to CLYDE.)

And your name is?

CLYDE

Clyde.

ANNA

Will you have a drink with me, Clyde? And you too, Father Tom? And Grogan Senior?

(All accept her offer. MICK gets busy)

I have a question for you all. If you don't mind. I was exploring in the village yesterday, and I discovered a strange old ruin of a place. The Church of Saint Seymour.

(Out of nowhere comes a strong, deep, menacing organ chord. ALL except ANNA exchange meaningful glances.)

ANNA

Did I say something wrong?

GROGAN

Never mind them. Go on with it.

ANNA

But you're familiar with the church I mean?

CLYDE

Yes, we're familiar with it.

ANNA

Well, I barely managed to get the door open, the hinges were so rusty. Then once I got inside____ it was so dark____ cold and damp too____and a bad smell.

FATHER TOM

Were you afraid?

ANNA

Of what? An old empty church? I went in and found Saint Seymour's tomb. And of course____that's when I saw the pigs.

FATHER TOM

Ah, the pigs.

ANNA

Is it your church? Saint Seymour's?

FATHER TOM

I have nothing to do with Saint Seymour's.

CLYDE

We all have nothing to do with it.

ANNA

But you've seen the pigs, right? You know what I'm talking about?

JUNIOR

Of course, Anna, we know the pigs.

ANNA

I've seen tombs all over Europe. The carved figure reclining, sometimes with his wife; or I've seen some with cats and dogs and angels. But this one, three pigs standing on Saint Seymour's chest?

FATHER TOM

Your guidebook makes no mention of it?

ANNA

It only says Saint Seymour was martyred here in 1536.

CLYDE

The pigs are frightening, aren't they?

How much of our history do you know, Mrs. Duval? I'm told it's not taught much in the average American school. Irish history especially.

ANNA

I didn't attend the average American school. I know some history.

FATHER TOM

Mick, refresh the drinks for everyone.

> (MICK goes about fixing drinks and serves them in real time as FATHER TOM spins the yarn.)

Well now. Ya know of the Terrible Times we've had here with the English, our smiling, polite oppressors who had us under the heel of their boot for all those centuries. Saint Seymour is part of that. And you've heard no doubt of the British King, Henry the Eighth who got into a scrape with the Pope. Not about religion either, though that's what the stories say. That evil King Henry lusted not only for a new woman every other week, he lusted most of all for power and great wealth, and he saw his chance in the property and assets of the Roman Catholic Church. He didn't let anyone get in his way either, being as how he murdered one of our own glorious saints, Thomas Moore, who had tried to stop him. And then he went about establishing his own church with his own henchmen "priests," so-called. Bold and shameless, he took over and stole all our monasteries, and churches. He kicked all the monks out, murdered and tortured them. And then, lo and behold, he turned his attention to Ireland. Seymour was a Missionary "Priest," so called, of the Church of Ireland, sent here by that evil King himself, to convert our loyal Catholic population. He had some soldiers with him too, just to give him a bit of an edge.

ANNA

I'll bet Seymour was not so welcome in these parts.

FATHER TOM

This is where the legend begins, ya see. It tells us that "Saint" Seymour was treated with most deferential respect and courtesy by everyone in the village. We were a gentle and kindly people after all.

ANNA

Ah. And still are.

FATHER TOM

So, it came to pass that Saint Seymour was preaching one day on the rolling green hills out there, no more than a mile from this very place. So there he was, as the story goes, putting horns on the Pope, and talking up the British King and his wicked Church of Ireland, when, by mysterious circumstance, a herd of pigs was infected by a band of devils. Those deviled-up pigs attacked Saint Seymour, and drove him over the cliffs above the sea, where he plunged to his death on the rocks below. And while falling he was heard to shout out a curse ____or so they said it sounded like a curse, but in Latin so no one knew for sure.

ANNA

So the pigs on the tomb____ represent the devil pigs that killed Saint Seymour?

FATHER TOM

Yes. And by the way the soldiers of the King disappeared about that time as well. No trace of them was ever found.

ANNA

Oh, come on, Father Tom. The people killed Saint Seymour, and the soldiers.

FATHER TOM

Everyone said it was the pigs. That's the legend that has come down to us for four and a half centuries. I'll not counter it.

CLYDE

Legends here are as hard as the rocks out there below the cliffs.

FATHER TOM

And that wretched place where you found the pigs is a tomb of the so-called Church of Ireland. Saint Seymour is one of theirs ya know, not a True Saint of the Holy Church. However, we're a tolerant people, and allow the church to stand, empty and abandoned as it is.

JUNIOR

But that's not the end of it, Father Tom. Tell her about Brigid the Witch Woman.

GROGAN

Ah, Junior why get into all that muckity muck? You'll have Mrs. Duval here thinking we're a band of painted up yahoos.

ANNA

Brigid the witch woman?

FATHER TOM

It's another tale, come down through the years. Back around 1660 there was a woman here who was seen to have particular powers. She could heal disease. She could see into the future, and predict it right on the nail, and she often had conversations with the dead.

ANNA

So they killed her?

FATHER TOM

Not at all. She was honored in the village. Though some used the term "witch" to describe her.

ANNA

I can see that.

FATHER TOM

Whatever she was, she claimed that Seymour appeared to her. He told her as he was falling off the cliff he did indeed pronounce a curse, and that he was coming back someday to take his revenge on the descendants of the people here about.

ANNA

But you said it was the pigs that did it.

FATHER TOM

Did I? Well, who knows? It's all confused and mixed up in the misty past. In any event, the woman Brigid was terrified of Saint Seymour. He had apparently threatened to devour her.

ANNA

Did he?

FATHER TOM

Did he what?

ANNA

Did Saint Seymour devour Brigid the witch-woman?

FATHER TOM

Oh, no, Brigid died a different kind of death. One day she spontaneously burst into flames.

ANNA

That is different

FATHER TOM

Yes. So ya see there are those of us who believe the curse of Saint Seymour to be the real McCoy.

GROGAN

Oh, come off it, Father. It is not a real thing at all. It's just one of those silly superstitious stories that gets handed down over the years from blithering fool to idiot. Ain't that so, Mick?

MICK

I try not to think on any of it.

GROGAN

It's all a load of foolishness, Mrs. Duval. Sorry ya had to hear it. We'd best be getting along, Junior. The sun is getting low.

JUNIOR

(To ANNA)

Good-bye, Mrs. Duval. Anna. I'll see you in the morning then?

ANNA

In the morning.

JUNIOR

Stop by our place along about nine, and we'll take to the road.

GROGAN

(To JUNIOR — As they go out)

So you're planning to blow off the whole day? That'll be just a fine big help to me.

JUNIOR

I'll make it up to yuh___I will, don't worry___

(JUNIOR and GROGAN are gone)

FATHER TOM

Well, I'd best be makin' my getaway as well. Chalk me up there, Mick. It was a pleasure to meet you, Mrs. Duval.

ANNA

Nice to meet you, Father Tom.

FATHER TOM

Good-bye, Clyde. You behave yourself now.

(FATHER TOM exits)

MICK

Anybody want anything else?

(CLYDE and ANNA indicate "no.")

I'll be in the back then.

(He yawns and goes)

CLYDE

(To audience)

He'll be taking a nap back there, and say isn't it convenient how, in the wink of an eye, Anna and I are left alone?

(HE gets up, goes over to ANNA and attempts to kiss HER)

ANNA (Violently)

What are you doing?

CLYDE

Indicating that we're intimate friends. It's one of the best surprise tactics in the book of playwriting. You leave two people alone in a room, and suddenly ____ boom!

ANNA

God, I hate Irish plays.

CLYDE

Shawn Michael O'Mooney is a bit in love with you. I suppose I was just acting it out ____So ya don't think there ought to a little hint of a something going on between us?

ANNA

The chances of that, Clyde, are worse than never.

CLYDE

So be it. I'll not be one to force myself ____So then, what do you think of him? Shawn Michael I mean____

ANNA

He has to stop blurting everything out. This is a con game. Ya tell lies. You've got to be totally untrustworthy.

CLYDE

He is in a way too honest I'll grant ya that. Still he's learning ____Don't ya think maybe he's learning?

ANNA

Oh, who knows? Who cares? Want another drink?

CLYDE

Ah, well now let me ponder that out a bit. In a pub like this? In a play like this? How could Clyde ever refuse? He wouldn't, and so I won't.

(ANNA goes behind the bar. SHE knows where everything is, an efficient bartender. Looks like she's been here before.)

Do ya know his latest scheme for the ending?

ANNA

He tells me nothing. I think he's afraid of me.

CLYDE

Well, perhaps I shouldn't be mentioning it, but he says we need a huge surprise saved up for the climax of the Second Act.

ANNA

Yeah? No kidding? That's like saying the pilot has a strong inclination to land the plane at the end of your flight.

(CLYDE is silent)

Oh, all right. What is it?

CLYDE

He wants to reveal that we're all actually ghosts, who don't know they're dead.

ANNA

Tell me I did not hear that.

CLYDE

No, it's true. He wants to reveal that we're all actually___

ANNA

Talk him out of it, Clyde, if you have any kind of influence.

CLYDE

Well now, I'm not sure I see it's such a drawback after all. Ghosts are a recurring theme in Irish plays.

ANNA

Irishmen are a recurring theme in Irish plays. Who gives a fuck? It's a god awful idea.

CLYDE

Well, yes, in a way, I suppose ___I'll communicate your concern to Shawn Michael. I'm sure he'll pay some attention to a creature of your vast experience. Remind me again exactly who you are.

ANNA

(Putting on a voice)

Remind me again exactly who you are. Jesus, Clyde that is such moldy cheese. Can't you slide in exposition any better than that?

CLYDE

There's no call for your turning snotty on me.

ANNA

Oh, sorry, sorry, sorry Mr. sensitive rose. Look Clyde, don't worry about who I am. Skip it. They don't care. Just say I am ___whatever ___existential! That sounds okay.

CLYDE

(To audience)

What she is of course, as some of you critics may have already discerned, is a prototypical character thought-form extruded from Jung's Universal Consciousness. She is the problematic, ambiguous, vaguely dubious and indeterminate leading woman, always attractive and while not evil, she is somehow compulsively destructive to herself and to others. She is a type consistently found in European literature, poetry and drama. She has many times occupied the position of goddess in the ancient cultures, even appearing often in the Bible. We're indeed fortunate to have her on our team tonight.

ANNA

Clyde, you are such a big suck-up.

CLYDE

I was only trying to give you a nice introduction. Would it kill ya to be pleasant for once?

ANNA

I am pleasant. I'm a pleasant, bright, lovable, mission-directed goddess. Now can we get back to work? We're here in an Irish play, God help us. Where does Irish drama come from, Clyde?

CLYDE

Uh _____? Come from?

ANNA

Irish drama comes from the world of nineteenth century theatrical realism. For some reason the Irish are still stuck back there about a hundred years behind the times. Oh, my goodness, this fourth wall is real, and we don't know we're in a play, and we take it all so seriously, all the thematic elements we deal with. And they are what ___by the way?

CLYDE

(Thinking hard)

Uh____

ANNA

You don't know your thematic elements?

CLYDE

Remind me why don't ya.

ANNA

Repression, Clyde. Repression is the first motivating thematic element of an Irish play. Religious, sexual, social And so this heavy repression leads us to what?

CLYDE

Uh ____a rolicking good story?

ANNA

Obsession. Everyone has an obsession, and it's gotta be destructive. Another thing, secrets and revelations, always exposed deep in the last act. Devastating, life changing. That's why Shawn Michael O'Mooney, the blabbermouth, has got to learn to keep a secret. I'm Anna but Anna is not really what she claims to be, yata yata ___. So later she reveals a stunning shocker, yata yata ___ the third thematic element: Confession.

CLYDE

Oh, yes ___Very important___

ANNA

Repression leads to Obsession, which leads to: Confession.

(CLYDE joins in reciting the formula)

ANNA

Okay, good, now let's get our heads into the second act. Pass this along to Shawn Michael. We've got an underused character, Grogan senior. I know he's scheduled to give the big memory speech where he tells us about the forty years ago lost love who ruined his life. But we oughta do more with him up front.

CLYDE

Noted. What about Mick though? I mean we're in good shape there at least. He has a really top of the line obsession, don't ya think?

ANNA

Mick has a gold-plated obsession. I'm bringing it out in the next scene.

CLYDE

(To audience)

Ah, what could it be? Mick's compelling obsession? We'll soon find out!

ANNA

Oh please, will you stop that!

CLYDE

Stop what?

ANNA

Talking to the audience. It annoys them.

CLYDE

It annoys them?

ANNA

They're smart. They get it. They see we're working on multiple levels here.

You don't have to rub their nose in it.

CLYDE

Shouldn't it be noses? Plural. Look out there. Do you see one nose or a multitude of noses?

ANNA

Ya want to know what I see? I'll tell ya what I see. Nothing____ but the fourth wall of the Horse's Glass Pub. And here is a window through which I see the muddy road running back up to the outskirts of the village. A light, misty rain is falling, as the late afternoon shadows deepen. I play by the rules, Clyde. I am a pivotal leading woman in an artfully conceived, serious and moving Irish play.

CLYDE

I see. Are ya now finished giving me attitude?

ANNA

As long as we're stopped, there's another thing.

CLYDE

What?

ANNA

Back at the beginning where you do that suck-up to the critics bit, where you obviously try to flatter them. That was embarrassing, Clyde. You don't think they see through you? They do, and it's going to backfire on all of us, and rain shit in our faces.

CLYDE

God, woman, do ya have you so little sense of humor? That was supposed to be comedy.

ANNA

It didn't strike me as funny. I thought it was just flat out stupid, and all that product plugging you were doing? Ford cars, Jameson whiskey. Where's your integrity, Clyde? I don't think you're taking this job seriously.

(CLYDE is silent)

Clyde?

(CLYDE is silent)

Well, what do you have to say for yourself, Clyde?

(CLYDE is silent)

See, the way it works. I say my line, and you respond. It's your turn to respond Clyde.

(CLYDE is silent)

You have to say something now.

(CLYDE is silent)

Anything____

(CLYDE is silent)

Say something, or I'm going to walk out of here, and leave you all alone.

(CLYDE is silent)

All right. That's it. Have a good time with your friends, the audience ____and their noses ____and the critics!

(CLYDE is silent)

I mean it, Clyde!

(CLYDE is silent)

Okay. Try entertaining them for thirty god dam minutes all by yourself.

(ANNA waits, no response. SHE storms out the main door, and slams it.)

CLYDE

(To audience)

Well, here's a development. What do ya want to bet she'll be back soon? What do ya think?

(ANNA comes back in through the main door.)

ANNA

I'm giving you one more chance.

CLYDE

Ya hurt my feelings.

ANNA

I hurt your feelings? Is that what I just heard? That's what this was all about?

CLYDE

Ya hurt my feelings. Coming in here, playing the boss, insulting my work, telling me I'm stupid. Ya hurt my feelings. That's the plain and simple black and white of it.

ANNA

The plain and simple black and white of it? Have you ever heard of the word: REDUNDANT?

CLYDE

Ya can take that up with Shawn Michael O'Mooney!

ANNA

All right. I have something to say to you, Clyde. Are ya ready? Say yes.

CLYDE

Yes?

ANNA

It's this. I apologize. If I hurt your feelings, I apologize. If I came on too rough and bossy, I apologize. If I seem to insult your intelligence, I apologize. If I unknowingly, somehow antagonized____

CLYDE

Aw, put a cork in it. Can we just get on with it?

ANNA

(Such dignity)

Very well____

                              CLYDE

All right then____

                              ANNA

All right then____

                              CLYDE

What do ya see for Father Tom?

                              ANNA

Father Tom ties in with my secret identity. I'll attack the Catholic Church___ I'll
destroy his faith.

                              CLYDE

I'm not sure he has any. Faith I mean. I've never heard him mention it.

                              ANNA

Does he have a horrible, guilty secret? He's got to.

                              CLYDE

If he has, he's doing a damn good job of keepin' a lid on it.

                              ANNA

I'll find a way to get at him. Ya see, Clyde, this ties in with something else we have
to think about. Father Tom would be an excellent candidate to take the dive off
the cliff.

                              CLYDE

What dive off of what cliff?

44

ANNA

Major resonating plot point. Somebody has to go off the damn cliff just like Saint Seymour. It's required, Clyde. It's inevitable. Must be in the play.

CLYDE

Oh, sure. I see what ya mean. How about the devil pigs reappear and drive everybody off the cliff?

ANNA

No, that's no good. The motivation has to come from inner psychic desolation.

CLYDE

Then the devil pigs drive 'em off the cliff!

ANNA

Oh fuck the devil pigs. That's a stupid idea, Clyde. Devil pigs! That was just the made-up story after they killed Saint Seymour. I trust we all know that.

CLYDE

We know it, and we don't care! Shawn Michael and me want the Devil Pigs. That's it.

ANNA

What do ya mean, that's it?

CLYDE

Shawn Michael and me, we out vote you two to one, even if ya are a goddess. What's your official goddess name by the way?

ANNA

(A thoughtful pause)

I happen to have the honor of being Dramanista, Goddess of Heroines.

CYLDE

(Sincerely)

Dramanista. Ah, that has a fine ring to it, it does. But we still want the Devil Pigs, Shawn Michael and me.

ANNA

I think you've convinced me of that, Clyde. Hooray! Devil Pigs it is. Now then, who goes off the cliff? I have two candidates — Junior, who's tragically mad for me, or, another possibility, you, Clyde____

CLYDE

Me?

ANNA

After I demolish your cause for existence, after I vaporize the very essence of your being, dashing yourself on the jagged rocks will look pretty damn attractive to you.

CLYDE

You're going to do all that to me?

(ANNA nods vigorously)

The audience won't like that at all. I'm too lovable.

ANNA

The audience doesn't give a rat's ass about you, Clyde.

CLYDE

Oh. How do ya know that?

ANNA

I know. It's my business to know.

CLYDE

Well ____ then rethinking what ya said, seeing myself as a heart-breaking, tragic hero sorta fella, if I did hurl myself onto the rocks, perhaps I could come back later in the climatic scene as a ghost?

ANNA

With a hot lavender light on your bloody mangled face! Ohooooeeee.

CLYDE

I'm only trying out ideas____

ANNA

Get him off this ghost thing. No ghosts in this damn play. They've been SO overused.

CLYDE

What about Shakespeare? His plays are crawling with ghosts. So I've heard.

ANNA

Darling Billy? He could get away with anything.

CLYDE

Ya knew him?

ANNA

Sure. He was a sweetie. But man, his language, like spaghetti in a blender. I could never figure out what he was trying to say. But we all pretended to get it____

(She takes a long pause)

CLYDE

What is it? Are you all right?

ANNA

You know what my trouble is, Clyde? I'm forcing. I'm forcing. I can feel it. I'm trying be this damn tragic motivator he wants me to be, and my heart is just not in it. Anyway, there's enough tragedy in the world already. Why couldn't we just do a big cheery old song and dance. God, I loved Greece. Ya know they invented musical theatre. And I was right there. I even wrote a couple of famous plays. Had to be a man to do it then, but being a man is not the worst thing I've ever done.

CLYDE

What is? I mean, is the worst thing you've ever done?

ANNA

I was a Vampire.

CLYDE

Ugh.

ANNA

Yeah. Exactly. Ugh. It was far worse than you could ever even begin to imagine, Clyde.

CLYDE

A vampire? That was a pretty long fall for a Heroine Goddess.

ANNA

Hey, we all slip up. Once in ten thousand years, you're allowed. Ya want another drink?

CLYDE

Yes I do. So what's it like, the lifestyle of a goddess?

ANNA

(Glides behind bar and pours drinks)

Sometimes they call me a Muse. I can go with that.

CLYDE

Muse. Has a pissed off sound about it. Muse! Have ya ever wondered why they need us?

ANNA

Why they need us? My dear, it's no mystery. They need us because they're stupid. They want to be writers. But they don't know what to write. We give them their ideas, and most of the time they don't even know we exist. They go on the talk shows and call it inspiration.

CLYDE

Shawn Michael believes in you, in a way___.

ANNA

Some of the brighter ones do. I'm working with a smart woman in Milwaukee right now. Her name's Monica Moran. She's making a little no-budget horror movie, of the bloody, disgusting type.

CLYDE

About a serial killer no doubt.

ANNA

Of course. Doctor Bob, the psycho dermatologist. He cures his patients by removing their skin. I'm creative advisor to the whole production and coaching Doctor

Bob's wife. In the showdown scene, Doctor Bob attacks her with a handheld food processor. I counter with a shotgun, blasting Doctor Bob in the face.

CLYDE

I like gross-out movies. Did you ever see the one where the serial killer turns out to be a Christmas tree?

ANNA

A Christmas tree?

CLYDE

Full of rage he is from bein' uprooted and decorated.

ANNA

Being decorated drives him over the edge?

CLYDE

Yes, he strangles his victims with his branches.

ANNA

(At the bar)

I'll have to file that one away. Have another drink?

CLYDE

So all the myths are true, you're all booze hounds____

ANNA

Most of the myths are true.

CLYDE

Yeah, nasty unnatural sexual stuff, I've read those stories.

ANNA

Oh, come on. Unnatural? There's no such thing____. Ya do what ya gotta do with whoever ya gotta do it. There's a song there ____

CLYDE

Did ya all live up on the top of that big mountain in Greece?

ANNA

No, that was one of those rare untrue myths. We hung out in a much better place, Clyde. An endless palace made out of pink clouds, floating high above the ocean where it was always sunset. Gorgeous music inhabiting your soul, and whatever you desired, all you had to do was think it. Whatever or Whoever You. Desired. And then when you got tired of continuous, total delight, you could go down to earth and become human. Did ya ever wonder, Clyde, why our most beautiful gods come down to earth time after time and wind up getting murdered?

CLYDE

We'll have to get Father Tom to explain it all for us.

ANNA

You're so bad____

CLYDE

Will you see that movie-making woman in Milwaukee anytime soon?

ANNA

Monica? Yeah, I'm planning to look in on her soon as I finish with Mick. Why?

CLYDE

Aw, I don't know. Be careful with that Doctor Bob, fella. There's something smells like bad fish to me there.

ANNA

Bad fish?

CLYDE

It's just a foreboding I have. Probably nothing.

ANNA

Oh, shit___ Foreboding in an Irish play? That's bad news___

CLYDE

Probably nothing.   I shouldn't have mentioned it. Be seeing ya!

(CLYDE gives her a nod and a wave, as he goes. MICK appears from the back room, rubbing his eyes)

ANNA

(To herself)

Bad fish?

MICK

You want anything?

ANNA

Did you have a restful nap?

MICK

No. Bad dream woke me up.

ANNA

I helped myself to some whiskey. I hope you don't mind?

CLYDE

Long as ya pay for it.

(ANNA places money on the bar.

ANNA

Here ya go. Keep the change.

MICK

(Grabs her wrist)

Thanks a bundle. Now then, what's your game?

ANNA

(Pulling free)

What's with you?

MICK

Like I want to know who you are and what yer doing here?

ANNA

My husband and I are going to build a factory. We are in the wireless broad band micro-chip software business. And you grab me that way again you'll be short handed.

MICK

Aw stuff that. Do ya take me for some kind of great, blithering child?

Who sent you?

ANNA

Who sent me?

MICK

What did they say about me? Somebody told ya something about me didn't they?

ANNA

No.

MICK

I suspicion that yer some kind of investigator they hired. To check out all the vile stuff they say, those bad mouthers down in the village? I could name names. I know who they are.

ANNA

I'm glad one of us knows.

MICK

Aw you'd naturally deny it. Wouldn't you?

ANNA

Deny what?

MICK

Nothing. Well, call it a draw then. Forget I mentioned anything at all.

ANNA

Wait a minute. What the hell is the vile stuff they say about you?

MICK

You know.

ANNA

I do not.

MICK

Sure ya do. Go on____

ANNA

They're saying ____Mick's a grand fella, but he gets a little zoned out sometimes?

MICK

They say I murdered my wife.

ANNA

Gee, I was way off wasn't I? Is it true then? You murdered your wife?

MICK

Haven't ya heard what I've been tryin to tell you? I did not. I deny it entirely.

ANNA

Well ____Okay. That's good then____

MICK

And you're saying nobody sent ya here to spy me out?

ANNA

Nobody sent me to spy you out.

MICK

Well, all right, let's leave it at that then. Benefit of the doubt, that's what I'll give yuz ____

ANNA

So, Mick, what is it they say about you?

MICK

Maybe you don't want to hear any of it.

ANNA

Of course I do. After all this build-up?

MICK

They say hard things.

ANNA

Such as?

MICK

Oh, I don't know, things like ____I came home one night and found 'em in the big tub together ____enjoying a bubble bath ____my wife and her friend ____all soaped up and slick ____and they say things like ____I must've lost my temper at the terrible sight of 'em____

ANNA

They say that do they? The terrible sight of 'em?

MICK

And they say things like maybe I picked up the electric heater meaning only to strike 'em with it ____only to scare 'em _____only to hurt 'em maybe a wee little bit____

ANNA

A controlled response.

MICK

Yeah. And they say the damn heater slipped and fell in the water, blew out the power in seven houses up and down the road. And they say when the officers of the Guard arrived, there were no bodies here, and it is speculated that I buried them in the dirt basement of this very place. And I say it was just coincidence that my wife went missing that night ____and so did her friend.

ANNA

Truth is stranger than fiction.

MICK

So there's no evidence against me. None at all. Only talk. It's his family that lead the bad mouthers. They'd like to see me hung. Only last week there was a fire out back. Lucky, I snuffed it or this place would've been ashes. You'll notice I never admitted to anything. I only reported the gossip.

ANNA

That you did. Tell me one thing, Mick, do ya have uncomfortable dreams?

MICK

No. Well, sometimes I see the two of them. Like just now when I was havin' my nap. You didn't hear me cry out did ya?

ANNA

No.

MICK

I saw the two of them. They looked ____like they're dead____. Laughing at me. Then I wake up. But that's not admitting to anything. They've disappeared, that's all.

ANNA

Some part of you must believe they're dead.

MICK

I don't know that for sure. I'm thinking ____ It's possible____ maybe they was kidnapped.

ANNA

Both of them?

MICK

Yeah, that's right. Maybe they was kidnapped.

ANNA

You ought to offer a reward then, for information leading to the arrest of the kidnappers.

MICK

Yuh. A reward.

ANNA

It's gotta be depressing for you, Mick, your wife gone ____and her friend ____and you falsely accused. Have they contacted you?

MICK

Who?

ANNA

The kidnappers. About a ransom.

MICK

(Thinks it over)

Not yet.

ANNA

Not yet, huh?

MICK

No. Not yet.

(A slight pause as each thinks his or her own thoughts)

ANNA

Look at that gray mist rolling in. You can't even see the field across the road ____
that same field from which the devil pigs drove Saint Seymour to his death.

MICK

The wind is picking up____.

ANNA

Yes. It's picking up____

MICK

Always picks up about this time of day. Wind from off the ocean. My Gran used to say ___when I was a wee lad___ She'd tell me it was the howling voices of the drowned sailors.

ANNA

Would she now?

MICK

From down deep in the ocean depths. That's what she used to say.

ANNA

(As lights start a slow fade)

So ___according to your Gran ___ the moans and the cries of the drowned sailors give the wind a voice. And the wind sings a tale of watery death__

MICK

Yuh. Watery death_____

(ANNA freezes in position, looks at MICK for a long time. Finally, the lights fade to black.)

End of **Act I, Scene 1**

ACT I

SCENE 2

(The Horse's Glass, about twenty-four hours later MICK is alone behind the bar, looking long and hard at something he alone can see. Dreamy lighting indicates late afternoon. GROGAN enters.)

GROGAN

Hey there, Mick.

(MICK does not speak)

I'll have me usual.

(MICK draws a dark pint and shoves it at GROGAN.)

Fearsome hot day today wasn't it?

MICK

Hot enough.

GROGAN

Ah, that tastes good. Beer tastes good when it's hot.

MICK

What?

GROGAN

I said: Beer tastes good when it's hot.

MICK

You're implying my beer's hot?

GROGAN

No, no, Mick, you misapprended me. What I was sayin' or meant to be sayin' was that cool beer tastes good when the weather is hot. That's all I was sayin'. Tell me have ya, by any chance, seen Junior anywhere today? Has he been in yet?

MICK

He hasn't been in at all.

GROGAN

He came to the shop this morning. That Mrs. Duval stopped by and picked him up. I haven't seen a breath of him since. What do ya think of her, Mick?

MICK

(After thinking it over)

She's all right.

GROGAN

Yeah, she's all right. Pretty sexy though. That is to say, I can see how Junior would get all wrought up over her. It's a bad thing though, her a married woman and all. I hope he keeps a square head. I worry a little bit that he hasn't been around today. And her neither? You haven't seen her at all?

MICK

No.

GROGAN

Well, that makes me wonder. Where they could be?

MICK

God only knows.

GROGAN

Well now, you'll get no arguments from me on that point, Mick. "God only knows" is a Theologically correct observation. I've often said to myself, Mick keeps a tight lip, but he thinks deep thoughts.

(MICK just looks at him)

You're doing it now aren't ya?

MICK

Doing what?

GROGAN

Thinking deep thoughts.

MICK

Is that intended as a remark on my domestic arrangements? "Deep" thoughts, is it? Deep? As in a grave? In the basement? Are you trying to be funny?

GROGAN

No, not at all. Listen, Mick, take no account of any of that talk that goes round. It's mean gossip, that's all it is. Pay no mind. Your domestic arrangements are your own private business between yourself and your wife, wherever she may be. And I truly hope she's safe and well.

MICK

So do I.

GROGAN

It's sorry I am for all your troubles.

MICK

All right, then.

(FATHER TOM enters)

FATHER TOM

Good day, Mick. Good day, Grogan. What's all right?

MICK

Everything's all right.

FATHER TOM

Everything's all right? Oh, I'm so pleased to hear that.

(FATHER TOM sits and studies his newspaper. MICK goes about drawing his regular and takes it to his table.)

GROGAN

I don't suppose you've seen Junior today, have ya at all, Father Tom?

FATHER TOM

No, I can't say that I've seen Junior today. Why do ya ask?

GROGAN

He went traipsing off this morning with that Mrs. Duval, and I haven't seen either of them since.

(FATHER TOM studies his paper.)

FATHER TOM

Yuz worried about him?

GROGAN

A wee bit anxious is all.

FATHER TOM

Ya ought to be. She can't help what she is.

GROGAN

And what is that?

FATHER TOM

As taught by the Church, "An Occasion of Sin."

GROGAN

Well now, I wouldn't exactly say that. She's a nice enough lady after all.

FATHER TOM

Indeed, she is a nice lady, and there's the trouble in a nutshell. She can't help it. She's a daughter of Eve, as are all women. When they cross their legs, they close the gates of Hell.

GROGAN

Well, I hope Junior didn't____ ya know _____try to venture through the gates____

FATHER TOM

We can only hope and pray. Here's a story that may be of interest to you, Mick. Old house in Dublin, they're excavating the basement for a remodel. Two bodies, well actually two skeletons are found. Believed to be two British agents from 1920, probable victims of Michael Collins.

MICK

And why do ya see fit to quote that story to me?

FATHER TOM

I thought it was an interesting thing. That's all.

GROGAN

A very interesting thing. Time of the troubles and all that. And do ya notice the young people today, why they have no idea of what went on then. They would say: Who's Michael Collins? And him the great Irish hero.

FATHER TOM

A hero to some. Others might call him a mad dog killer.

GROGAN

Oh? Is that a fact?

FATHER TOM

Not that I would ever say such a thing____

MICK

Here now! Both of yuz. We'll not be refighting the old wars here.

FATHER TOM

I make no further comment.

GROGAN

Nor will I, but it was tragic all the same. Here we had fought the British to a bloody stump, then we had to get a civil war going to kill our very own selves. Awful stupidity it was.

(A beat of silence)

FATHER TOM

I make no further comment on political matters.

MICK

Good news for you, Grogan.

(Pointing out the window)

Yer boy just drove up. There, ya see. He looks all right.

FATHER TOM

Saints be praised.

GROGAN

Mick, do me a favor, will ya? Pour his usual, so as to have it waiting for him when he walks in. I'm that glad to see him. She's not with him is she?

MICK

(As HE fixes drink)

No. Remind me again____

GROGAN

Jameson neat. Water on the side. Well, I'm glad he's here. He's a good lad. I'm relieved.

FATHER TOM

So are we all.

(JUNIOR enters. HE looks all around, nods curtly then sits at the empty table opposite FATHER TOM. JUNIOR radiates misery. MICK takes his drink to the table.)

JUNIOR

What's this?

MICK

Your usual. From your Da.

GROGAN

On me, son. I'm that glad to see ya.

JUNIOR

I don't want it.

MICK

Ya don't want it?

JUNIOR

Thanks. I'm grateful and all that, but I don't want it.

MICK

It's your usual.

JUNIOR

Ya know what I want, Mick? I want an unusual. I want the most rotten, ugly, drink you've got.

MICK

Ya really do?

(JUNIOR nods. MICK nods. He's game for it. HE drinks down the Jameson with gusto, then goes back behind the bar and gets busy. He chuckles and sings a bit as he putters back there.)

FATHER TOM

That's a rather unique kind of request ya just made.

JUNIOR

I'm a rather unique kind of bloke.

GROGAN

What is it, boy? What's wrong?

(JUNIOR just looks at him)

Does this have anything to do with that Mrs. Duval?

JUNIOR

It's torment to be in love like I am, with no chance in hell.

FATHER TOM

Hah!

JUNIOR

What would you know about it, ya damn unnatural man?

GROGAN

Junior! He's a priest after all.

(Note: MICK has gone in the back room briefly, then comes back)

JUNIOR

Sorry. Sorry. I'm not feeling myself at all____

FATHER TOM

I'm a priest but I do understand carnal obsession. As priests we're not immune to it. I take no pride in saying that. Priests are always falling down in their vows, be it with women or men, boys or girls. We're all sinners under the skin, and that's the truth of it. Junior, do ya need to go to confession?

JUNIOR

I have nothing to confess. Except that I love her. That's all. Real, deep and true. I love her. There's no sin in that.

FATHER TOM

Lusting after another man's wife? Don't I recall that violates one of the Ten Commandments?

JUNIOR

Alls I did was hold her hand.

FATHER TOM

Ya held her hand? She let ya hold her hand? That's how it starts.

GROGAN

(Admiring)

She let ya hold her hand?

JUNIOR

For the longest time, as we were driving along. Me chattering away. The wind blowing her hair. Both of us laughing. She has that effect on me. When I'm with her I know everything. I'm full of bright sayings. Even jokes. I'm free as the breeze. Ya ought to see me. I'm really sorta charming. She said as much.

(MICK places a glass in front of him)

MICK

Here's what ya ordered, Prince Charming.

JUNIOR

What's that?

MICK

The most ugly drink I've got.

JUNIOR

I asked for that?

MICK

Ya did. Drink it down.

GROGAN

I would strongly advise you not to drink that, Junior.

FATHER TOM

I would second that advice.

MICK

Go on, it's what he asked for.

JUNIOR

What's in it?

MICK

I tell ya that only after ya drink it. That's the house rule for this here particular kind of cocktail.

JUNIOR

It's a cocktail then is it?

MICK

You might say that.

JUNIOR

I don't believe I want it now.

MICK

Ya ordered it up. What are yuz? A coward? What would yer lady friend say if she was here?

(JUNIOR answers with action. He grabs the glass and downs the drink all in one gulp.)

JUNIOR

Jesus! Argh!

(JUNIOR stumbles out to the toilet, slams the door. HE can be heard barfing.)

GROGAN

(To FATHER TOM)

I'll tell ya one thing. I dread asking the question. But I dread more hearing the answer. What was in that?

MICK

What was in it?

GROGAN

Yes, what was in it?

MICK

Mostly milk____

GROGAN

Milk?

MICK

Sure, it was Milk. Well aged milk. Been in the frig since New Year's Day.

GROGAN

This is June!

> (JUNIOR appears at the door of the toilet, wiping his mouth with a towel.)

MICK

And then I added a little something extra special to it.

GROGAN

What?

MICK

(Gesturing appropriately)

A personal something of me self. I went in it.

GROGAN

Ya went in it?

MICK

Just a wee bit. Hah!

> (JUNIOR, hearing this, gags again, and is back to the toilet
> room)

GROGAN

Ya oughta be ashamed, Mick. That's a terrible thing to do to a loyal customer. How long have we been coming here? Two generations, regular as clockwork. I'm most disapproving of your behavior. I am. Truly so.

FATHER TOM

Just think on it, Mick, what if ya did that to everybody who comes in here? Business would go downhill fast.

> (CLYDE enters from the outside door)

GROGAN

A very nasty trick. Oh, I'm sure ya meant it as a joke, but not funny. Not funny in the least.

CLYDE

What's going on?

GROGAN

Mick pissed in Junior's drink.

CLYDE

Ugh. You don't mean to say?

GROGAN

I do. A bad nasty thing.

(JUNIOR returns, sits. Mick pours a glass, takes it to him.)

MICK

Here, drink it. On the house. Sorry. It seemed a funny idea at the time.

JUNIOR

Yeah? You're a man who's little known for comedy.

MICK

To repeat. Sorry. I must have been a little bit daft. Maybe Clyde is getting to me.

CLYDE

Sure, put it off on me.

JUNIOR

(Sips the drink)

What is this?

MICK

By way of apology, to wipe out the other taste. Maker's Mark, Kentucky bourbon whiskey.

JUNIOR

That's very good. Or maybe it's only by way of contrast with what went before.

MICK

Naw, it's really good stuff.

JUNIOR

It's my new usual. Never forget that.

(He offers his hand to MICK. THEY shake. The main door now opens and ANNA appears. SHE carefully studies the scene, waves to CLYDE who returns a slight nod. JUNIOR comes up to ANNA.)

JUNIOR

Anna. Hello.

ANNA

(Sweetly)

Hi ya, Junior.

JUNIOR

I'm so sorry over what happened. Me makin' a fool of myself that way.

ANNA

(A bit distracted, being kind)

Forget it. These things happen. Are you okay? You're all white.

JUNIOR

I'm fine. I'm fine. But what happened ____it shouldn't have happened. I ought to learn to keep a better check on my instinctive emotions. Wild as they are.

ANNA

(SHE might pat him on the cheek)

We'll talk.

(SHE dismisses JUNIOR and sits down with CLYDE)

CLYDE

We've in serious trouble here. He just pulled the oldest bar joke in the history of the world.

ANNA

The oldest bar joke? That would be: Mick pissed in somebody's drink?

(CLYDE nods "yes.")

Yuck. Who was the lucky guy?

CLYDE

Junior.

ANNA

Aw, poor Junior. He's had a tough day.

CLYDE

So ya do see what we're up against here?

ANNA

We're dealing with a well-meaning incompetent.

CLYDE

Of course, when ya think of it, everyone's well meaning.

ANNA

Well, I've made up my mind, Clyde. I'm outa here. What about you?

CLYDE

I'm not at all sure____ There could be, perhaps, some hope____

ANNA

There is no hope Clyde. We're wasting our time here. We've both got better things to do. I could be in Milwaukee tracking Doctor Bob, the murdering sonofabitch. You could be the critic's darling in some compelling, piece of horseshit.

CLYDE

That's all true, I guess. Still I'll hate to see ya go, Goddess Dramanista.

ANNA

We'll work together again sometime. Hey, we're both professionals, right?

CLYDE

And proud to be.

ANNA

These things happen. I've seen it a thousand times. He'll leave this play unfinished, put it in a drawer. Twenty years later he'll read it ____put it back in the drawer____

CLYDE

Uh ____by the way, what should I tell the others?

ANNA

I handle my own dirty work, Clyde.

(SHE rises from the table and speaks to everyone)

Uh ____time out. Time out. Listen up, everybody. I've come to a decision. I've decided to bail out of this thing. I don't mean to sound harsh. Shawn Michael O'Mooney is good-hearted and well-intentioned. I'm sure of that, but in his sincere attempt at writing an Irish play he has made one fatal blunder after another. The blunders are you.

GROGAN

You're calling us blunders?

ANNA

I am. I'm sorry, but none of you has what it takes. Are there any tragic obsessions that lead to inevitable destruction? Are there any in this room? Are there any horrid secrets to be revealed in the last scene?

(They think this over)

I thought not.

MICK

Hold on, now. What about me falsely accused of having two murdered bodies interred in the basement?

ANNA

But Mick, you are so perfectly comfortable with it. Don't ya see? It doesn't gnaw at your guts. It doesn't haunt you. Ya may or may not be a murderer, and ya put on a grumpy face, but you're as happy as a birthday cake.

FATHER TOM

May I remind you that I will ultimately be exposed as a living lie. Lost my faith in God and the Church, even as a youth. But I fancied the comfortable life of a priest. So here I am, lazy, rotten with hypocrisy, and I'll confess to all of it ____whenever you're ready.

ANNA

Anyone can spot you for a fraud. Who cares? Nobody cares.

JUNIOR

I am tragically in love with you. My heart aches with longing. I am doomed.

ANNA

You're just a healthy guy with a hard on.

(SHE goes up to GROGAN)

Grogan, what can I say? I like you, man. But I don't find you dramatically compelling. Okay?

GROGAN

I've got the story of a lost love I can tell

ANNA

Lost love? Grogan, my dear, give me a break. I know you're all ready to roll. Twenty minutes of overstuffed memory monologue. And the bottom line is, ya only saw her once, and your bus was goin' East, and her bus was goin' West, and there's not a day that passes that you don't think of her, and what could've been.

GROGAN

It's touchin' the way I tell it. Brings a tear____.

ANNA

I'm sure. Look, don't get the wrong idea, that I think the less of any you. You're all grand people in your own ____special way, it's just that he doesn't have a clue as to how to squeeze maximum value out of you, which leaves me in a hell of a bind as the motivating character. You all know that he planned to have me reveal myself to you as the reincarnation of Saint Seymour, here to avenge my death at the hands of your ancestors. And he was going to try some stupid thing with the devil pigs. You all knew that?

FATHER TOM

I had some inkling of it.   I was trying to twig out how I would relate to you as a pagan goddess, but then since I've lost my faith, who gives a rip?

ANNA

Well, there you've said it____ Who gives a rip?

FATHER TOM

But I was wondering one thing though____

ANNA

What?

FATHER TOM

Seeing how you're a goddess and all. Do you know any of the famous people of the Bible? The Saints and Angels and such? Not that I believe in that stuff anymore ____ It's all lies. But just in case it's true, have ya ever met Himself? The big guy?

ANNA

Which big guy? The Father? Or the Son?

FATHER TOM

Ah, never mind. You're scaring me now.

ANNA

Out of that Family my favorite is Third Person, the one who turns himself into a dove. Or a lick of flame.

FATHER TOM

The Holy Spirit? Are ya sayin' ya actually know The Holy Spirit?

ANNA

I asked him once, how do you decide whether to turn yourself into a bird or a fire? I really wanted to know. Professional curiosity.

CLYDE

And he said?

ANNA

"It all depends."

> (ANNA dances to some unheard music as she flounces out through the main door.)

That's it. Goodbye fellas. Lots of luck. See ya around.

CLYDE

> (Calling to her)

Give 'em hell in Milwaukee! Nail that Doctor Bob!

> (ANNA exits)

JUNIOR

She's gone. I'll never see her again.

CLYDE

Face it boys, she was too polite to say so, but we're a team of duds.

JUNIOR

I'll never see her again.

GROGAN

Now, now Junior, have a glass of your new usual. I'm buyin' for everybody. Let's not get down on ourselves. Let's bolster our spirits.

FATHER TOM

(In his own world)

The Holy Spirit. The Holy Spirit said: It all depends. I see it. I see the true meaning there. It all depends! She was a messenger from the Blessed Trinity. Not a goddess, but an angel, sent here among us to work a miracle! Glory to God, my faith is restored!

(HE falls on his knees. The others ignore him.)

CLYDE

Yup, we were tried and found wanting. She had a better story to work in. A movie chasing a serial killer. How could the likes of us match up with a serial killer?

GROGAN

It's proud I am not to be a serial killer. If she's too high and mighty for us, well so be it, let her go. There can be plays about good, dull, normal people. Can there not? There's enough badness in the world without making plays about it. Perhaps, after all, Shawn Michael O'Mooney is on to a new thing.

CLYDE

There's no such thing as a new thing.

FATHER TOM

(Still on his knees)

Didn't anyone here take note how my faith was restored?

GROGAN

(Passing him off)

I'm sure we're all very happy for ya, Father Tom. Best get up now. You'll get the knees of yer trousers dirty.

(FATHER TOM gets up, goes to the bar)

MICK

I see it coming. No ya don't get a drink on the house because your faith was restored.

(FATHER TOM looks at him)

Aw, screw it!

(HE pulls a pint for FATHER TOM)

JUNIOR

We're not sad enough. We're not rotten enough. We're not fucked up enough. We're not mean and hard enough.

CLYDE

Not obsessed enough.

JUNIOR

That too I suppose____

CLYDE

Obsession to Repression to Confession.

JUNIOR

Not frightening enough. Not disgusting enough. Well, no, that's a lie. After that cocktail Mick gave me.

MICK

Yuh, I'm the only one here who's really trying.

CLYDE

(To audience)

So ya see where we're at. The crises moment. The dark with no dawn in sight. If this was a submarine movie_____ We'd be stuck on the ocean floor. The enemy above us dropping water bombs, and us mad with fear, our bodies dribbling sweat.

(BOMB sound goes off. Everyone reacts shaking, falling over, acting it out.)

CLYDE (Cont.)

And the lights flickering____

(Lights flicker, bombs continue)

And then the submarine springs a leak!

(A squirt of water from offstage hits MICK directly in the face.)

MICK

All right now! That'll be enough of that!

CLYDE

Merely demonstrating the crises moment. The rule is: Show, don't tell.

MICK

Well, you've shown enough.

GROGAN

I've got a really chilling ghost story I could tell. If I proceed at a deliberate pace, it takes twenty minutes to get through it.

JUNIOR

Which will seem like twenty years.

CLYDE

Yeah, put a lid on that one, Grogan, she's down on ghost stories.

GROGAN

This is the one where we all turn out to be ghosts ourselves. And who the hell cares what she thinks about it? She's gone. She took herself outa the game. It's up to us to carry on, boys. Let's go! Let's get the old blood up!

(There is a moment of thoughtful silence)

CLYDE

How did we die?

GROGAN

What?

CLYDE

I said ____if we're all going to be ghosts ____how did we die?

GROGAN

We were sitting around, like we are now, just talking away. Ya know? Just like in real life. And something happens, that turns us into ghosts.

CLYDE

Ya may be on to something, Grogan. When ya consider, it is after all, the ultimate, plot point. Death. When ya introduce old Mister Death into the story line there's no one can accuse you of not being serious. The critics always appreciate death.

JUNIOR

Perhaps then, if we all did something really, really, stupid, and insanely self-destructive, she'd come back to us for the end of the Second Act.

CLYDE

When we've been turned into ghosts. Yeah, and that in itself will piss her off ____ which could be a good thing. Can ya imagine the scene? She comes back and finds us all turned into ghosts. I can hear her now: "Ya idiots, I told ya to cut out the ghost crap!"

JUNIOR

She turns me on when she's pissed off.

(A strange, scuffling noise comes for offstage, and then the sound of hundreds of pigs going oink oink oink ___)

MICK

What the hell is that?

(MICK dashes to a window.)

JUNIOR

It sounds like____

MICK

Pigs. Hundreds of 'em out there.

FATHER TOM

Pigs?

CLYDE

(Looking out another window)

Over here as well.

JUNIOR

(Joining CLYDE)

They must have the building surrounded.

FATHER TOM

It all depends____

CLYDE

Their eyes. Do ya notice their eyes?

MICK

Unnatural, terrible eyes____

CLYDE

Red eyes, burning with rage____

FATHER TOM

(In another world)

I see. Yes, I see. The pigs are a symbol____

CLYDE

(To audience)

Devil pigs surrounding the Horse's Glass. Kind of reminds me of a scene in that movie, THE BIRDS. Except here of course, the pigs are not on the roof. At least I hope they're not. Pigs with wings is a bad idea.

MICK

They're callin' to us, those pigs, they're sayin' come on out, boys, and play with us.

GROGAN

They're saying: "We mean ya no harm."

JUNIOR

Play with us? What does that mean?

MICK

It's the message I'm pickin' up through my brain waves.

FATHER TOM

You're getting messages from the pigs?

MICK

They're sayin' we got em all wrong. They're not evil. They're friendly. They want us all to come out and join in ____a frolic. That's what they're sayin'. They want us to frolic with 'em.

CLYDE

That's crazy, Mick! Have any of you ever seen a pig frolic? They don't frolic. They roll in the mud!

MICK

Could be I misinterpreted the word? But they're nice enough little fellas, even if they are pigs. I'm goin' out there.

GROGAN

I'll go with ya, Mick. We must never judge a pig by the fact it eyes are red. They can't help the color of their eyes. We must look pretty damn strange to them as well.

JUNIOR

Da, is that such a good idea after all? They look dangerous to me.

GROGAN

(Ignoring JUNIOR)

Clyde, are ya comin'.

CLYDE

(To the audience, grinding out the words in disgust.)

Bad ideas. The thing about em is, they always come at you in disguise. They come dressed up as good ideas.

(CLYDE joins GROGAN and MICK. The three of them go out the main door. JUNIOR hangs back a moment, then bolts after them. FATHER TOM stands up, has face a mask of indecision, then he resolves himself.)

FATHER TOM

Oh, God, I'm afraid. But they're my people. My place is with them! May the Holy Spirit guide and protect us!

(HE crosses himself and heads for the door as the pig sound builds and lights fade to black.)

END OF **ACT I, Scene 2**

ACT II

SCENE 1

(Lights up, The Horses Glass, six months later. JUNIOR is seen behind the bar. He is studying a book, and writing on a yellow pad. The woman we knew as ANNA enters, looks around. SHE wears an attractive buttoned up rain coat.)

JUNIOR

Hello.

ANNA

Hi there____

(SHE continues to gaze all around)

JUNIOR

Can I get ya something?

ANNA

(As SHE continues to study the place)

I'll have a lager ____dash of lime.

JUNIOR

(As HE pulls the drink)

So, a bit warm for December, eh?

ANNA

What?

JUNIOR

I said we're having a warm December.

ANNA

What are ya reading?

JUNIOR

Oh, just a book ____a book I found____.

(HE shows her the book)

ANNA

"*Tricks of the Playwriting Game.*" By Shawn Michael O'Mooney.

JUNIOR

I'm thinking about maybe ____trying to ____ya know____

ANNA

Well, of course, this is Ireland. You're all poets and playwrights, and song writers. Oh, don't mind me, I'm just a wide-eyed tourist, taking it in for the first time. What's it's about? Your play.

JUNIOR

I haven't even tried to start it yet. It'll concern itself with something that happened here.

ANNA

Here?

JUNIOR

(After a lengthy pause)

In this very place. I take it you've never heard of____?

ANNA

I just got in today.

JUNIOR

You've heard no one mention____?

ANNA

I saw your cute sign. The Horse's Glass. No, no one mentioned anything____

JUNIOR

Well, the memory still goes down hard with me. I thought perhaps if I could write about it ____If I could get it down ____on paper ____ya know?

(JUNIOR chokes back tears.)

ANNA

Aw, come on, it can't be that bad. May I buy you a drink?

JUNIOR

So that's the first thing out of the box is it? Buy me a drink? Of course, why not? It's Ireland after all, the land of drunks.

ANNA

I was trying to be____

JUNIOR

That you were. That you were. Sorry. Let it go. Let it go____.

ANNA

Hey ____? Are you all right?

JUNIOR

I'm tip top.

ANNA

Good. Pour yourself one.

(JUNIOR pours himself a Maker's Mark neat)

Maker's Mark, that's nice stuff. Goes well with beer.

JUNIOR

Yuh. I used to drink Jameson's. Long ago. With a little water on the side. It was my usual. But Mick could never remember ____My Da, it was funny, he always had to remind him. Always had to remind Mick ____Now they're both gone____

ANNA

Gone?

JUNIOR

Six months ago ____to this day exactly ____five men walked out the front door of this pub. Their names ____well, their names would mean nothing to you. But they were observed ____all of them ____running as if being pursued. Running in terror is how one witness described it. Actually, there were a hundred and fifty witnesses. And they all described it the same.

ANNA

That's a hell of a lot of witnesses.

JUNIOR

It was the Foley family reunion-picnic. A yearly thing. Held out there in the meadows near the cliffs of Saint Seymour. So these five fellas were seen by the whole

Foley clan, running in terror, and yellin' and screamin' as how they were being pursued by a band of Devil Pigs.

ANNA

Devil Pigs?

JUNIOR

Yes. And then all five of them took a dive off the Cliffs of Saint Seymour____

(JUNIOR is having trouble now, fighting back tears)

And four of them crashed onto the rocks below, and their bodies washed out to sea, never to be found.

ANNA

You're saying five of them dived off the cliff, but only four of them were killed? What happened to the other____?

JUNIOR

You're lookin' at him.

ANNA

Oh, my God_____

JUNIOR

I jumped off with the rest of 'em, one of them being my own father ____my own Da____

ANNA

Oh, no____

JUNIOR

Was it good luck or bad? My braces got hooked in the branches of a tree outcropping the rocks. One of the Foley's, being an expert mountain climber, had his ropes and the spikes in back of his Ford Explorer. He climbed down, as they tell me, hooked me up and pulled me to safety. I have no memory of it. I woke up in the hospital, and the doctor informed me of it all.

ANNA

And your name is ____?

JUNIOR

Grogan O'Brien Junior. They call me Junior.

ANNA

Happy to meet you, Junior. My name is Beverly Boppo.

JUNIOR

It is? You're sure it's not Anna_____ or something like that?

ANNA

It's Beverly Boppo.

JUNIOR

If you say so. Well. It's a pleasure to meet ya____ Beverly. Excuse the emotionalism just now.

ANNA

(SHE takes his hand)

And you have no memory at all? Of why you were running? Why you dove off the cliff?

JUNIOR

They say we were running to escape the Devil Pigs, which were invisible to the Foley family. It's an old legend. There was a preacher, back in the fifteen hundreds. He was British, Protestant, most unpopular. The people rose up and flung him off the cliffs out there. The Cliffs of Saint Seymour. Only the ones who did it, put out the story that a herd of pigs had gone wild with the devil in them, and run old Saint Seymour over the brink. I've given up trying to make sense out of any of it. One minute I was sitting here with my Da, having my new usual. The next I knew I was waking up in the hospital.

ANNA

That's quite a story.

JUNIOR

Do ya ever get that feelin'_____ Beverly? Ya meet somebody for the first time, and yet they seem to be immediately like an old friend?

ANNA

Like you've known each other forever?

JUNIOR

That's the truth of it entirely. As if ya can almost hear in your head what they're gonna say next.

ANNA

Means you've known them in another life.

JUNIOR

Ah, I don't twig to that stuff. One lifetime here and I'm gone for good and all.

(ANNA sips her drink)

So, Beverly, you're from the states? What part exactly?

ANNA

Milwaukee, Wisconsin.

JUNIOR

What do ya do back there?

ANNA

Investigative Research. People hire me to find out things.

JUNIOR

Ah then, ya must be brainy.

ANNA

Just a matter of asking the right questions. For example, I wonder how you came to wind up here? Doing this? After what happened to your father.

JUNIOR

Well now, it just sorta worked itself out. I'm a distant cousin to Mick's wife.

He was the Publican here. The owner. He took the fatal plunge with my Da.

His wife, the one who's my distant cousin, was in Dublin at the time, stayin' with a lover man. They'd run off with each other some months before. It's funny, well no, it's more sad than funny. There had been quite a lot of silly talk in the neighborhood, accusing Mick of murdering his wife and her lover man. They said he buried them in the basement. So anyhow the lover man left her in the lurch in Dublin. There was nothing for her but to come back and make a go of this place. She had lost her husband. I had lost my Da. She took pity on me I suppose, and here I am.

ANNA

What ever happened to that Ford dealership you had?

JUNIOR

Oh, my heart was not in it. And there was a ready buyer for the business. I came out fine.

ANNA

So now you can indulge yourself playing the Publican ____like Mick____

JUNIOR

Say now, I don't recall that I told you about that Ford business. Did I?

ANNA

Sure you did.

JUNIOR

(Phone rings, HE picks up)

Horse's Glass ____Yes? ____ This is the place. How many? ____You know there's a cover charge? ____Right ____A little before sunset is the best time for them to come ____You know I make no promises ____Yes, there is adequate parking for the bus. And it's cash up front, Irish or dollars, no credit cards, no euros__ Right. See ya then.

(HE hangs up)

ANNA

Business picking up?

JUNIOR

Twenty-five German tourists. Not bad.

ANNA

Coming here? With a cover charge?

JUNIOR

They'll pay it or they don't get in.

ANNA

But why?

JUNIOR

You know why don't ya? Some way or other this has all happened before. We've met before. We're old friends from way back aren't we? Why not admit it?

ANNA

Why are twenty-five German's coming here this evening, Junior? Not for a gourmet dinner that's for sure. As I remember Mick didn't even keep a loaf of bread behind the bar.

JUNIOR

Once he had a great hunk of cheese. It lasted well over a year.

ANNA

Right. So what's the deal here, Junior?

JUNIOR

So happy I am that you came back. I was always hoping you would, my dear Anna. I still have the same feelings for you____

ANNA

Stop.

JUNIOR

All right. However ya want to play it, Anna, Beverly, whatever ya want to call yourself this time. The sight of ya still thrills my heart.

ANNA

Oh, Junior, you're hopeless.

JUNIOR

That's me. Mister Hopeless. Here, let me top ya off there.

(He refills her glass)

A hopeless, tragic case. A mortal man hung up in love with a cruel goddess.

ANNA

I am not cruel. I just have a little edge, that's all. Why are the German's coming?

JUNIOR

I've been puttin' off tellin' ya about it.

ANNA

No kidding____.

JUNIOR

Fearing you'll have a downer reaction.

ANNA

A downer reaction?

JUNIOR

When ya hear.

ANNA

Hear what?

JUNIOR

All right. All right. The twenty-five Germans are comin' here to enjoy the genuine
Irish Ghost Experience. There. Every evening and into the night this pub is haunted
by three of the men who took that header off the cliffs. Clyde, Mick, and my own
Da. Sometimes they appear to the customers. Sometimes they don't. Some nights
there's only heavy breathing and a chill in the air. Sometimes glasses break, spilling
all over the customer's pants. Sometime a sickening odor can be smelled wafting
out of the toilet room.

(Pause. ANNA says nothing)

JUNIOR (Cont.)

Ya know, I did expect ya to have more of a blow-off here. You were always so down
on the whole ghost scheme. Remember how ya used to scorn and make fun of it?

ANNA

Only three of them?

JUNIOR

That's right.

ANNA

Whatever happened to Father Tom?

JUNIOR

He went on.

ANNA

He went on?

JUNIOR

To Heaven. Oh, you can laugh, but that's how I see it. He appeared to me in a dream, only a week after. He was wearing a white linen suit, a white silk shirt, and a red tie. He said the Holy Spirit was teaching him how to turn himself into a dove, and he demonstrated the trick right there in the dream.

ANNA

Such a sad guy, he was. I hope he's found peace.

JUNIOR

Peace and Happiness seems to be the whole idea of the place. After he converted from the dove back into himself, and he told me an amazing thing. It turns out he was a saint.

ANNA

A saint?

JUNIOR

All along. A Saint. Not the kind recognized by the Church of course, but the Holy Spirit Himself, told Father Tom, that he was a special type of saint. The kind who reads his newspaper and drinks his pint every day, and causes no harm to anyone. That's all it takes to be a saint these days.

ANNA

Apparently. Well ____good for him____

JUNIOR

So ya don't mind it after all, them turning out to be ghosts at the end of the end.

ANNA

It's not a question of whether I mind; or whether I approve. Who wants my opinion? Not Shawn Michael O'Mooney, that idiot. He does as he pleases____ like all writers. We work for them, Junior. They tell us what to do. We do it. End of discussion.

JUNIOR

(With love)

Why do ya sound so bitter?

ANNA

(Fighting back tears)

They use us and abuse us, and when they're done with us ____That bitch Monica Moran, after everything I taught her_____

JUNIOR

(The THREE GHOSTS appear from behind a trick panel in the set, just as audience focus is drawn to JUNIOR and ANNA)

Aw, come on Goddess, no tears ____no tears now____

ANNA

(Spots THE GHOSTS)

Oh, hi, fellas. I never wanted to see you finish up this way. Remember? I warned you ____Didn't I warn you?

CLYDE

You made that clear, Goddess Dramanista.

(They hug)

Good to see ya again, my dear.

ANNA

So ya lost all control over him, Clyde?

CLYDE

Yuh, that's right, I'm afraid. When the devil pigs appeared, my influence went bollicks up.

ANNA

You're the one who wanted them ____as I recall.

(A handshake with GROGAN)

Hello again, Grogan.

GROGAN

Goddess Anna. It's not so bad, this ghostly life. I don't really mind, taking it one day at a time. Each day like yesterday and tomorrow like today____ How was Milwaukee?

ANNA

Horrible. Horrible. I should never have left you guys ____ Big mistake____

GROGAN

Ah, well ____too bad is too bad. Have a drink. We never have to pay.

MICK

Sure, have a drink and cheat on me wife.

ANNA

So you were innocent after all, Mick.

MICK

I always said, didn't I?

ANNA

You always said. That ya did. But what about that Father Tom, huh? A Saint after all.

JUNIOR

And sometimes a dove.

GROGAN

A dove, maybe. I can see that. But a saint? Come on ____I never saw him being all that extra special good ____Of course I never saw him as much of anything____

CLYDE

Excuse me for a moment. There's something I have to do.

(Directly to the audience)

Well. So here we are, winding up the play in a cocked-up crumbling shambles. Three of us are ghosts, and one of us is in heaven which sounds a dreadful place, based on the clothes they make ya wear. It's what I call hitting the bottom with yer face to the mud. Oh, and don't expect to see any German tourists comin' on to save the day. Ya think this shabby play could afford twenty-five extras? And likewise don't look for good old Saint Father Tom to come flying in on the wings of a dove in some kind of impossible special effect, happy, feel-good inspirational flim-flam. No, we're done. We're cooked and the meats fallin' off the bone. We're at a great awful train wreck smashed up all over the damn stage, thanks to the gross and stupid fucktitude of Shawn Michael O'Mooney.

GROGAN

Well said, Clyde. You spoke for all of us there, I think.

ANNA

Does anyone want to hear what happened to me in Milwaukee?

CLYDE

It was not so hotsey-totsey?

ANNA

It was bad fish, you said it yourself.

CLYDE

I did?

ANNA

It was the director's idea. He was Monica Moran's cousin, a graduate of the Summer School Film Production course at the University of Wisconsin.

CLYDE

So he was well qualified.

ANNA

He threw out the whole last scene. He said Doctor Bob could not be killed. He must survive our final confrontation to be able to star in the sequel.

CLYDE

What a great director!

ANNA

Oh, barf on you Clyde. Doctor Bob grabbed the shotgun out of my hands and blasted me in the chest with it. Want to see the grim result?

CLYDE

No thank you.

> (SHE faces upstage, and throws open her raincoat.
>
> ALL react in horror. ANNA spins around and shows the audience.
> Her chest is a masterpiece of makeup effects. A bloody mass of
> destruction, featuring shattered bones, glistening, bloody chewed
> up flesh. SHE is a disgusting, bloody shock!)

See the work that a twin shotgun can do! Fuck you, Doctor Bob! Fuck you Monica Moran, you sicko, sell-out slime-weasel bitch!

GROGAN

Ah ha. Look, out there, the bus is pulling up.

CLYDE

I'm sorry, Goddess. Truly I am.

ANNA

After all I did for her. I wind up like this?

JUNIOR

It really looks truly awful and shocking, Anna. Good job, if that helps any____

ANNA

But you still love me. Right, Junior? Come, give me a big hug____

(JUNIOR backs off fearfully.

> (SHE refastens her raincoat.)

JUNIOR

That's all right, Anna. We can understand your hurt feelings.

ANNA

That's no excuse to act like a damn vampire. I apologize, Junior.

GROGAN

Ya know, there's something familiar about that fella just got off the bus. Looks like he's headed this way ___.

> (THEY wait a beat, and then the main door opens. In comes FARADAY FLYNN who was last seen as FATHER TOM.)

FLYNN

So this is it, eh? The spook pub. You must be Junior?

JUNIOR

I am.

FLYNN

Faraday Flynn is the name. Leprechaun Coach-Travel Service. I've got twenty-five Germans out there, waiting to come in here.

JUNIOR

They'll be most welcome.

FLYNN

Oh, I'm sure they will be. But we have a little deal to cobble up first.

JUNIOR

A deal?

FLYNN

I take a skim off the top of their bar bill. Let's say twenty percent?

JUNIOR

Let's say nothing of the kind. Let's say ten percent.

FLYNN

At ten percent I keep 'em here three minutes, and then we're off. Good luck to ya.

JUNIOR

It takes awhile for the ghosts to appear____

FLYNN

Oh, I'm sure it does. What have ya got? Projectors, sound machines? I hope it's all professionally done and not too embarrassing.

JUNIOR

There are no machines. These are real live ghosts.

FLYNN

The hell ya say?

JUNIOR

It's no shenanigan. One of them is my own father.

FLYNN

Well, there's a twist for ya. Listen, ya can't be playing games on these people. These are hard headed Germans. Ya hear me? They're not to be arsed about with. I'll go at thirteen percent if you show me they're real ghosts.

JUNIOR

They're real!

FLYNN

Oh, yuh? Prove it.

JUNIOR

What?

FLYNN

I said ____prove it ____that's they're real ghosts.

JUNIOR

I don't know how to do that.

(GROGAN goes up to JUNIOR and whispers in his ear.)

All right. All right then. Close your eyes and count to ten ____slowly. When ya open them ____you'll see ghosts.

GROGAN

Gather around now____

(ANNA, CLYDE, MICK and GROGAN gather around FLYNN.)

FLYNN

One____

ANNA

So how do ya do this?

FLYNN

Two____

CLYDE

Just sorta bear down ____in your gut ____like when ya go to the bathroom.

FLYNN

Three____

ANNA

Oh ____like when ya have a baby____?

FLYNN

Four____

JUNIOR

I love ya Anna! You can do it!

FLYNN

Five____

ANNA

I can do this. You bet your ass I can do this____

FLYNN

Six____

CLYDE

Up yours, Shawn Michael O'Mooney!

GROGAN

Steady now____Steady____

FLYNN

Seven____

MICK

Prepare to shit yer pants ya little cock flogger!

FLYNN

Eight____

> (ANNA steps forward, whips open HER raincoat, takes position
> on front of FLYNN.)

CLYDE

Oh ____yes ____Goddess Dramanista! Give it to him! Give it to him!

FLYNN

Nine____

> (CLYDE, MICK, GROGAN, and ANNA all scream together)

FLYNN

Ten____

> (HE opens his eyes, horrified, runs out the main door screaming.)

JUNIOR

Now he'll never bring them in here_____

ANNA

Hey, he asked us to appear. We did! Bugger off!

CLYDE

And so say all of us!

ANNA

Man, that felt good! Like I've got my balls back.

MICK

It's proud I am to be on your team, goddess whatever your name is____

GROGAN

Wait a minute ____Look____

JUNIOR

Holy Glory. They're coming off the bus____ They're coming off the bus!

GROGAN

What do ya all suppose the theme of this play has been all along____?

MICK

Essentially life-affirming I would say. All about friendship____

CLYDE

Yes, and the great universal truth that life goes on, even under strange and altered circumstances.

ANNA

Life goes on? That's it?

JUNIOR

Here they come. Here they come. I must say, Anna, you do make a super frightening ghost.

ANNA

Thank you for that, Junior. I'm feeling better now.

JUNIOR

And your little disability makes no matter to me, I'll forever love ya.

ANNA

Aw, that's sweet of you ____Come here, Junior.

(SHE plants a big kiss on JUNIOR)

JUNIOR

(In a daze)

That was worth livin' a lifetime for_____

(ANNA holds JUNIOR in her arms, as they rock slowly back and forth.)

CLYDE

(To audience)

Well, there you have it. A life-affirming theme which also demonstrates the power of family, friendship and abiding love.

MICK

Jesus, yes, they ought to give us credit at least for uplifting intentions. After all there's more than enough tragedy in the world already.

(The GHOSTS position themselves around the room, ready to receive company.)

ANNA

(ANNA comes down and speaks to the audience)

We started out small with a little amateur production at the Village Community Theater. Then, on to Dublin, then to London, with me whisperin' in the ears of the critics, with mostly happy results. Only a few insulting reviews to make it seem authentic. Then, Glory Be a great big fat hit in New York where the critics love anything that's Irish, all of which led to the television pilot, and the six-part

ANNA (continues)

HBO miniseries. Sean Michael O'Mooney brought it to Los Angeles, with me helpin' him run the shows. Now we've just moved into a house in the Hollywood Hills. And with us, of course, his lady love, she of the high cheekbones, and pale blue eyes and big white teeth who plays me in the series. We're joined by Clyde sometimes, as we develop a new TV property. It's all about a plastic surgeon from Milwaukee who, when the moon is full, turns into a Christmas tree.

(ALL on stage freeze, music stings as lights fade to black)

Printed in the United States
By Bookmasters